O 8/19 Never

Boo Crew

Don't miss a single

Nancy Drew
Clue Book:

And coming soon:

Nancy Drew

✶ CLUE BOOK ✶

#10

Boo Crew

BY CAROLYN KEENE ✶ ILLUSTRATED BY PETER FRANCIS

Aladdin

NEW YORK   LONDON   TORONTO   SYDNEY   NEW DELHI

This book is a work of fiction. Any references to historical events, real people, or real places are used fictitiously. Other names, characters, places, and events are products of the author's imagination, and any resemblance to actual events or places or persons, living or dead, is entirely coincidental.

ALADDIN

An imprint of Simon & Schuster Children's Publishing Division
1230 Avenue of the Americas, New York, New York 10020
First Aladdin paperback edition September 2018
Text copyright © 2018 by Simon & Schuster, Inc.
Illustrations copyright © 2018 by Peter Francis
NANCY DREW, NANCY DREW CLUE BOOK,
and colophons are registered trademarks of Simon & Schuster, Inc.
Also available in an Aladdin hardcover edition.
All rights reserved, including the right of reproduction in whole or in part in any form.
ALADDIN and related logo are registered trademarks of Simon & Schuster, Inc.
For information about special discounts for bulk purchases, please contact Simon & Schuster Special Sales at 1-866-506-1949 or business@simonandschuster.com.
The Simon & Schuster Speakers Bureau can bring authors to your live event.
For more information or to book an event contact the Simon & Schuster Speakers Bureau at 1-866-248-3049 or visit our website at www.simonspeakers.com.
Series designed by Karina Granda
Book designed by Nina Simoneaux
The illustrations for this book were rendered digitally.
The text of this book was set in Adobe Garamond Pro.
Manufactured in the United States of America 0818 OFF
2 4 6 8 10 9 7 5 3 1
Library of Congress Cataloging-in-Publication Data
Names: Keene, Carolyn, author. | Francis, Peter, 1973- illustrator.
Title: Boo crew / by Carolyn Keene ; illustrated by Peter Francis.
Description: First Aladdin hardcover/paperback edition. |
New York : Aladdin, [2018] | Series: Nancy Drew clue book ; #10 |
Summary: Nancy Drew and her friends investigate when strange things start happening at a local theater, rumored to be haunted, during auditions for a televised talent show.
Identifiers: LCCN 2017049037 (print) | LCCN 2017059524 (eBook) |
ISBN 9781534413900 (eBook) | ISBN 9781534413887 (pbk) | ISBN 9781534413894 (hc)
Subjects: | CYAC: Theaters—Fiction. | Haunted places—Fiction. |
Actors and actresses—Fiction. | Mystery and detective stories.
Classification: LCC PZ7.K23 (eBook) | LCC PZ7.K23 Bq 2018 (print) | DDC [Fic]—dc23
LC record available at https://lccn.loc.gov/2017049037

✻ CONTENTS ✻

Chapter

READY, SET, SHOW!

"Double, double, toil and trouble!" George Fayne declared. Then she wrinkled her nose and said, "Did witches really talk like that?"

"They spoke that way in William Shakespeare's play *Macbeth*," eight-year-old Nancy Drew said. "I'm glad my dad told me about the old play so we can audition as the three witch sisters!"

Nancy's best friend George rolled the big black cauldron up the street. Her other best friend, Bess Marvin, helped Nancy carry a duffel bag filled with witch costumes and awesome brew ingredients.

George blew dark curly bangs out of her eyes. "'Bubble, bubble' sounds better than 'double, double,'" she said. "Why don't we say that instead?"

"We will have a bubbly cauldron of brew," Bess said happily, "thanks to my bottle of strawberry bubble bath!"

"Then 'bubble, bubble' it is!" Nancy said.

If the girls' hands weren't so full, they would have high-fived. The hit show *Twinkling Little Stars* was coming to River Heights to audition kids for their TV talent contest.

"I'm glad the auditions are for their special Halloween show," Nancy said. "We get to dress up two weeks before Halloween!"

"I hope the judges like our brew ingredients," George said, nodding at the cauldron, "toenail of toad, scale of dragon, tooth of giant—hairball of cat!"

"Ewww," Bess cried. "I'm glad all that stuff is fake—it's totally gross."

"Speaking of gross," George said excitedly, "I'm going with my mom later to see the movie *Zombie Slime Monsters*!"

"*Zombie Slime Monsters*," Nancy repeated. "Is it true the movie theater will serve slime-green popcorn?"

"Only for the special five o'clock show," George said. "Can't wait!"

Bess stuck her tongue out and made gagging sounds. "Slime-green popcorn? I'll stick to crunchy caramel!"

Nancy giggled and said, "Are you sure you're cousins?" You're as different as—"

"Slime-green and caramel popcorn?" George joked.

Bess used both hands to grab the handle of the bag.

"This bag is getting heavy," she said. "Why do we have to drop off our costumes and props today? It's only Friday, and the auditions are Saturday and Sunday."

"Everyone auditioning has to, Bess," Nancy said. "It's the contest rules."

The girls were glad to reach the theater where the auditions would be held. The Heights Theater was old-timey but looked brand new with a fresh coat of paint and a shiny gold front door.

"I wonder if we'll meet the judges today," Nancy said as they filed inside.

"I can't believe Lucy O'Toole is one of the judges," George said. "I think she's the funniest comedian, and she grew up right here in River Heights."

"And I can't believe the other judge is the actress Cookie Sugarman!" Nancy said. "Can you believe she's only nine years old and is supposed to be the sweetest star in Hollywood!"

"Even Cookie's movies are sweet," Bess said. "I saw *The Princess and the Unicorn* three times!"

"*The Princess and the Unicorn*," George scoffed.

"That movie was so sweet I had to brush my teeth three times!"

Bess rolled her eyes at George. "Who's the third judge, Nancy?" she asked.

"It's the owner of this theater," Nancy replied. "I think his name is Nathan."

"Who wouldn't want to own this place?" George asked as they looked around the lobby. "It's awesome!"

Plush red velvet chairs and sofas stood on golden-colored carpeting. Covering the walls were posters from long-ago shows.

"It looks like a fairy-tale castle," Bess said, pointing upward. "Even the ceiling is painted blue with white clouds!"

Nancy couldn't believe her eyes either. The old Heights Theater had just reopened after being rebuilt. The *Twinkling Little Stars* auditions would be the first event there in more than seventy years!

"Do you believe this building used to be old and creepy?" Nancy said. "We even thought it was haunted!"

More kids walked by holding costumes and props. One was Quincy Taylor from the girls' third-grade class. Quincy held a mummy costume as he stopped to face the girls.

"Who says this theater isn't still haunted?" Quincy asked them.

"What do you mean, Quincy?" Nancy asked.

"You heard about the curse, didn't you?" Quincy asked. "About a hundred years ago an actress named Nora Westcott starred in a play here. Nora was mad when the director replaced her with a bigger star."

Quincy lowered his voice almost to a whisper. "The director didn't know that Nora was also a witch!"

"We're witches too," Bess said with a smile. "Bubble, bubble, toil and trouble—"

"Nora was a real witch," Quincy cut in, "and there was trouble all right."

"Trouble?" Bess asked.

"The Heights Theater has been haunted ever

since Nora's curse," Quincy answered. "By ghosts and monsters!"

"Not true!" a deep voice said.

The kids turned to see a tall man with dark hair standing behind them.

"I am Nathan Alonso, the owner of this theater," the man said. "The only thing that ever went bump in the night was when a clumsy stagehand dropped a set piece."

"So there are no ghosts or monsters?" George asked.

"Zero, zip," Nathan insisted. "Zilch."

Quincy smiled. "You've got to be right, Mr. Alonso," he said. "No ghosts or monsters here. Whew, what a relief!"

Nathan walked away. The girls turned to Quincy with surprise.

"What made you change your mind so fast, Quincy?" George asked. "Because he's the owner of the theater?"

"Because he's one of the judges and I want to

win!" Quincy said. "Hey, I may be a mummy, but I'm no dummy!"

As Quincy walked away, Bess turned to Nancy and George, her blue eyes wide.

"What if Quincy's right?" Bess asked. "What if this theater is filled with monsters and ghosts?"

"Quincy is always talking about ghosts," George scoffed. "He's a member of that goofy Ghost Grabbers Club."

Bess nodded. "Yes, remember when they tried to help us solve the mystery of Murray the Monster Mutt?" she sighed. "They weren't much help."

"Who cares about grabbing ghosts?" Nancy asked with a smile. "I like our own club, the Clue Crew!"

As the Clue Crew, Nancy, Bess, and George solved mysteries all over River Heights. Nancy even owned a clue book where she wrote down all of their suspects and clues.

"Quincy can look for ghosts if he wants to," George said as she rolled the cauldron. "I want to find the prop room so I can park this pot!"

Nancy, Bess, and George followed the others down a hall to a large room. Inside, kids were busy hanging up costumes and placing props on shelves.

"There's Shelby!" George said, pointing to their friend Shelby Metcalf from school. "She's juggling monster eyeballs!"

A few feet away was another kid wearing a hairy werewolf mask. Nancy recognized Kevin Garcia's voice as he told monster jokes. . . .

"What's a werewolf's favorite bedtime story?" Kevin asked. "A hairy-tale!"

Kevin threw back his head and howled, "Ah-woooo!"

Nancy wasn't surprised to see their friend Nadine auditioning for *Twinkling Little Stars* too. She was the best dancer and actress in Ms. Ramirez's third-grade class.

"Is that a spider costume you're hanging up, Nadine?" Nancy asked.

"Not just any spider," Nadine said. She turned to three other kids hanging up the same costumes.

"We're Cirque du Crawl-ay, and we're dancing with a giant spiderweb!"

"Break a leg, Nadine," George said. "All eight of them!"

Across the room a small crowd was watching Antonio Elefano, dressed as a vampire. The girls traded smirks. If Nadine was the class actress— Antonio was the class pest!

"Tell me, Mr. Fang," Antonio asked a bat puppet on his hand, "what is a vampire's favorite snack?"

Antonio used his other hand to lift a glass of grape juice to his lips. While he gulped it down the puppet said, "Scream of tomato, Count Joke-ula. Yum!"

"Pretty neat," Bess admitted. "How did he do that?"

"I don't know," Nancy admitted, "Since when is Antonio such a good ventriloquist?"

Suddenly George pointed to the floor underneath Antonio's long cape. "Hey!" she said. "Since when do vampires—have four feet?"

Chapter

2

TROUBLE BREWING

"Four feet?" Nancy repeated.

She, Bess, and the others looked down to see where George was pointing. Peeking out from beneath Antonio's long cape were not one—but two pairs of sneakered feet!

"Busted," Peter Patino groaned as he stumbled out. Peter was Antonio's friend. But probably not for long.

"You and your big feet, Peter," Antonio muttered.

"So Peter was making Mr. Fang talk," Kendra Jackson called out, "Not Count Joke-ula!"

"Antonio Elefano, you cheated!" Shelby complained.

A woman dressed in a white blouse and black pants walked over. "I'm Sherry Hemmings, the producer of *Twinkling Little Stars*," she said. "I just saw what happened."

"So?" Antonio asked with a shrug.

"So having your friend talk for you wouldn't be fair," Sherry said. "Why don't you try throwing your voice by yourself, like ventriloquists do?"

"But we're a team," Antonio argued. "Partners!"

"Partners in crime," George mumbled.

"Heard that, Georgia Fayne!" Antonio snapped.

Nancy could hear George suck in her breath. She hated her real name, Georgia, more than sweet movies about unicorns!

"What have you decided to do, Antonio?" Sherry asked.

Antonio gulped down the rest of his juice,

wiped his mouth with his bat puppet, and said, "Thanks, Ms. Hemmings, but we'll take our amazing act—elsewhere!"

As the boys pushed past them, Nancy heard Peter say, "Let's go for pizza."

"Go without me," Antonio said glumly. "I've got a messy job to do."

Nancy wondered what that messy job could be. But her thoughts were interrupted when Mayor Strong walked into the room. Everyone gasped when they saw who the mayor was with.

"I'm sure the judges need no introductions,

kids," Mayor Strong said. "Meet Lucy O'Toole and Cookie Sugarman!"

"Omigosh!" Nancy gasped. "It's them!"

In a flash the kids crowded around Lucy and Cookie.

"I am so thrilled to be back in River Heights!" Lucy exclaimed. "I want to do everything I did when I was a kid . . . except clean my room."

Nancy giggled along with the others. Lucy was her favorite comedian too.

"And I can't wait to judge your auditions this weekend," Cookie said with a smile. "Oh, I wish I could vote for each one of you right now!"

"Isn't she sweet, kids?" Mayor Strong asked, then quickly added, "and our third judge is Nathan Alonso, the owner of this theater."

Nathan opened his mouth to speak, until Sherry stepped forward and spoke first. . . .

"Auditions for third-graders will be held here tomorrow morning," Sherry announced. "Fourth-graders will audition Saturday afternoon and fifth-graders on Sunday morning."

Before anyone could get selfies with Lucy and Cookie, the stars were whisked out of the room. After making sure their costumes and props were put away, the girls left too.

"Meeting Lucy and Cookie was awesome," Nancy said.

"Tomorrow will be even awesomer," George said. "I'm so happy we're in the third grade—because that means we get to audition first!"

Bess stopped walking to look up at the cloud-painted ceiling. "Wait," she said, "do you hear that? It's coming from upstairs.

All Nancy heard were kids leaving the theater. "Hear what, Bess?" she asked.

"Someone just laughed," Bess said.

"Laughs are good," George said.

"Not this laugh," Bess said. "Instead of ha, ha, ha, it was more like mwah, ha, ha! Like a mean monster laugh."

"Monster?" George shook her head. "Bess, do you still think this theater is cursed by a witch?"

Bess flicked her long blond hair and said, "Maybe."

"You heard what Nathan told us, Bess," Nancy said gently. "There are no monsters or witches in this theater."

George flashed a smile. "Except three super-cool witches auditioning for the show tomorrow," she said. "Us!"

Bess smiled too as the girls chanted, "Bubble, bubble, toil and trouble! We'll win this contest on the double!"

"How was *Zombie Slime Monsters* yesterday?" Nancy asked George.

It was Saturday morning and the day of the *Twinkling Little Stars* audition. All three girls sat buckled up in the backseat of Mr. Drew's car, too excited to sit still.

"The movie was great," George said. "But the snacks—not so great."

"Why?" Bess asked.

"The slime-green popcorn machine broke down," George sighed. "I had to eat gummy bats instead."

Nancy saw her dad smile in the rearview mirror as he drove to the theater. "Are you sure parents can't watch the auditions?" he asked.

"Totally sure, Daddy," Nancy said. "Only kids are allowed."

"But you can wish us luck, Mr. Drew," Bess said with a smile. "That always helps!"

Mr. Drew wished Nancy, Bess, and George the best of luck as he stopped in front of the Heights Theater. The girls climbed out of the car, rushed into the theater, and hurried straight to the prop room.

"Look!" George said. "That door wasn't open yesterday."

Nancy looked through the door. It led directly backstage. Cool!

"Don't forget to put everything you'll need for your auditions backstage, kids," Sherry told everyone.

After pulling on their witch costumes, the girls carried and rolled their own props backstage. They found three empty seats in the theater and sat down.

"This looks different than a movie theater," Nancy whispered as they looked around.

"Smells diffcrent too," George whispered back. "No popcorn or nacho chips."

Lucy, Nathan, and Cookie were sitting behind a long table in front of the stage. Each wore a round white badge with the word JUDGF. in rcd letters.

Mayor Strong walked to the middle of the stage to a microphone. Nancy felt Bess squeeze her hand. This was it!

"Welcome, talented kids of River Heights," Mayor Strong announced. He pointed to the audience and said, "I'm talking about you!"

As everyone cheered, Cookie turned to give a thumbs-up. Nancy smiled. She really was sweet!

"Without further skid-doo—let's bring out an act that even Miss Muffet would love,"

Mayor Strong said. "Please welcome—Cirque du Crawl-ay!"

Nancy, Bess, and George clapped for Nadine and her friends. The spider-dancers sprinted onstage holding a big ropey spiderweb over their heads.

Music played as Cirque du Crawl-ay danced. But the faster they danced, the faster things began dropping down on them—squiggly black things!

"Ewwww!" one dancer shrieked. "There are spiders all over this web!"

More dancers shrieked, letting go of the web. The spidery net dropped over them in a big tangled mess!

"Get us out of here!" Nadine cried.

Mayor Strong and Nathan helped free the dancers from the web. The mayor picked up a spider and held it up for all to see.

"Don't worry, kids," Mayor Strong chuckled. "These spiders are rubber."

"We didn't put them there!" Nadine cried. "Somebody did it to ruin our audition!"

Nancy watched Cirque du Crawl-ay drag themselves and their web from the stage. Did someone really put the spiders in their web? And why?

"All right then," a frowning Mayor Strong said into the microphone. "Our next act will make you howl with laughter. Please give it up for Kevin Garcia."

Kevin ran onstage, his werewolf mask covering his head. His voice sounded a bit muffled as he told his first joke: "When do werewolves go trick-or-treating?"

Kevin waited a few seconds then said, "Give up? They go trick-or-treating—on Howl-a-Ween!"

As some laughed, Kevin began to howl, "Ah-wooo! Ah-wooo!"

But then he threw back his head and began to sneeze, "Ah-choo! Ah-choo!"

"Is that part of his act?" George whispered.

"I don't think so," Nancy whispered back.

Sniffing loudly into the mike, Kevin told his next joke: "Why can't mummies have fun? Because they're too wrapped up in their work! Ah-wooooo!"

Once again, the ah-woos turned back into ah-choos. A lot of ah-choos!

"Arrgh!" Kevin cried pulling off his hairy mask.

"Something inside this thing is making me sneeze!"

Nancy, Bess, and George traded worried looks. First Nadine's act flopped and now Kevin's? What was up?

"Nancy, Bess, George," Sherry called to them from the aisle. "Your audition is next, so get ready."

As the girls made their way backstage, Bess said, "What if something goes wrong with our audition too?"

"What happened to Nadine and Kevin was a bummer," George insisted. "But our audition is going to rock!"

"All we have to do is pour strawberry bubble bath over our brew stuff," Nancy said, "and we're all set."

But as Nancy poured the liquid into the cauldron, Bess said, "I don't smell strawberry. It's not pink either, it's green!"

"Girls, you're on!" Sherry called.

The girls hurried onstage with their cauldron and mixing stick.

"What's brewing?" Mayor Strong asked the audience. "Meet the three witch sisters and see for yourself!"

The girls stood around the cauldron. After a group cackle, Bess stirred the brew while all three recited their lines: "Bubble, bubble, toil and trouble. Fire burn and cauldron—"

Nancy glanced down and her jaw dropped. Their witchy brew was bubbling all right—all the way up to the rim!

"Eeek!" Bess shrieked as something green, thick, and soupy oozed over the rim. Nancy watched with horror as it crept across the stage toward the judge's table. Lucy, Cookie, and Nathan jumped up, backing away from the stage.

"If I knew I'd be taking a bubble bath," Lucy shouted, "I would have packed my rubber ducky!"

The bubbling brew simmered down as Shelby and Kendra ran out from backstage.

"Somebody poured glue on my monster eyeballs!" Shelby cried. She raised both hands to show eyeballs stuck to her palms. "How can I juggle like this?"

"And somebody cut the strings on my skeleton marionette!" Kendra cried. "How did this happen?"

A boy in the audience stood up. He was wrapped in white bandages like a mummy. Nancy knew it was Quincy

"I know why everything is going wrong!" Quincy declared. "It's the witch's curse on the Heights Theater!"

Nathan turned and shook his head. "I told you, kids," he said. "There are no curses or monsters in the Heights Theater!"

"Absolutely, Nathan. There has to be logical explanation for all this!" Mayor Strong agreed.

"When you find out, let me know," Sherry said firmly. "Until then, the auditions in River Heights are canceled."

Nancy stared at her two best friends. Canceled? Oh no!

Chapter

3

BOO CREW

Nancy, Bess, and George couldn't believe what they heard. Neither could the others, as everyone spoke at once: "No auditions?" "No trip to Hollywood?" "No starring on *Twinkling Little Stars*?"

"I guess that's a wrap," Quincy sighed.

Mayor Strong's arms waved in the air as he spoke to Sherry. "Please, Ms. Hemming," he said, "surely we can work something out."

"We're leaving River Heights on Sunday night," Sherry said, walking toward the door with

Lucy and Cookie. "I hope you can get to the bottom of this before then."

When Sherry and the judges were gone, Nathan made an announcement. The kids could keep their things in the prop room in case the auditions were held later in the weekend.

"Let's keep the cauldron here," Nancy said.

"Yeah," George said. "All that oozing made it look like a pot of boiled-over pea soup!"

The girls dragged the icky witches' cauldron back to the prop room. Most of the kids had already left, so the room was almost empty.

"Maybe Quincy is right," Bess said. "Maybe what happened was because of the witch's curse. I heard that evil laugh, remember?"

"Witches don't laugh, they cackle," George said.

"I have a feeling the spiders, sneezing, and oozing brew were done on purpose," Nancy said. "And not by a witch, a monster, or a ghost!"

The girls tried to shove the cauldron under a table against the wall. But it would only go so far. . . .

"There's something else under there," George said. She crawled underneath and dragged out a shopping bag. The bag was from the Rags 'n' Gags costume and novelty shop on Main Street.

"Rags 'n' Gags is where we got our witch costumes," Nancy said with a smile.

"They sell the coolest joke stuff too," George said as she stuck her hand deep inside the bag. "I wonder what's in here."

"Don't snoop, George," Bess said. "The bag doesn't belong to us, so it's none of our business."

"Oh yeah?" George said. "Check this out."

George pulled out a can and held it up. It was a can of Skeevy's sneezing powder!

"Sneezing powder!" Nancy gasped. "Maybe that was sprinkled inside Kevin's mask to make him sneeze!"

"What else is in there, George?" Bess asked.

George announced each item as she held it up: "One almost-empty bag of rubber spiders! A bottle of green Bubble Blast!"

"No wonder our bubbles were out of control!"

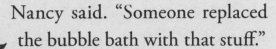

Nancy said. "Someone replaced the bubble bath with that stuff."

"So that's why I didn't smell strawberries!" Bess said.

The last thing that George pulled out was the sales receipt. Not only did it show the price, but it also showed the date and the time of the purchase.

"This stuff was bought on Friday at five o'clock," George said, reading the receipt. "That's after we dropped off our costumes and props here."

"Whoever did this was at Rags 'n' Gags at that time," Nancy decided. She turned to Bess and smiled. "See? Monsters, witches, and ghosts don't shop at stores."

"Unless they're boo-tiques!" George joked.

"But if it wasn't a monster or a ghost, who was it?" Bess asked.

"I don't have a clue yet, but I do have this," Nancy said. She reached into her backpack and pulled out a small book. "My clue book!"

Tucked inside Nancy's clue book was a pen with purple ink. Nancy used it to start a list of everything from the Rags 'n' Gags bag—the sneezing powder, rubber spiders, and bottle of Bubble Blast.

"Are you still here?" a voice asked.

Nancy, Bess, and George looked up to see Nathan Alonso.

Nathan looked at the book in Nancy's hands. "Are you girls doing homework?" he asked.

"No, but it is an assignment," George said as they walked over to Nathan. "Sort of."

"Maybe you can help us, Mr. Alonso," Nancy said, "by telling us how late the theater was open on Friday."

"There's no show at this theater yet," Nathan said, "so I locked the theater at five o'clock. After everyone dropped off their costumes and props."

"What time did you open this morning?" Nancy asked.

"I opened the theater at seven-thirty," Nathan replied. "I wanted to get here early, before the auditions, so I could do some work in my office."

"Was the prop room open early too?" Bess asked.

"It was," Nathan answered. He raised an eyebrow and said, "Since when do witches ask so many questions?"

"Oh, we're not just the brew crew," Nancy said with a smile. "We're the Clue Crew!"

"We'll be leaving now, Mr. Alonso," George said. "No more questions."

As Nathan walked back to his office, Bess said, "What do you mean, no more questions, George? We should have asked him about Nora's curse!"

"Nathan said there was no curse," George said.

"That was before all those weird things happened," Bess said. "Remember?"

Nancy was too busy writing the time line to talk about monsters or ghosts.

"Nathan locked the theater after everyone dropped off their stuff yesterday," Nancy said. "And he opened it early this morning."

"So the person who messed up our props," George figured, "must have been in the prop room early this morning too."

"If Nathan was here," Bess said, "wouldn't he have seen somebody in the prop room?"

"He might have been too busy in his office," Nancy said. "We should go to Rags 'n' Gags and find out who was there yesterday at five o'clock."

Bess spotted something on the floor and picked it up. It was a judge's badge.

"Nathan must have dropped his badge when he was here," Bess said, slipping it into her pocket. "I'll give it to him on our way out."

The girls left the prop room. As they made their way down the hall Nancy said, "Let's start a suspect list. Who do you think ruined the auditions?"

"Antonio was mad that he was caught cheating," George pointed out, "and wasn't allowed to audition the way he wanted to."

"He also said he had some messy job to do," Nancy said. "And what happened at the auditions was super messy!"

Nancy was about to write Antonio's name in her clue book when—

"Do you hear that?" Bess said, looking up at the ceiling.

"Not that monster laugh again, Bess!" George groaned.

"No," Bess whispered. "It sounds like someone is playing the piano."

"This is a theater, Bess," Nancy said, "Some shows have music. They're called musicals."

Bess shook her head. "Nathan said there is no show going on here now," she said. "I want to go upstairs and see what's up."

"Okay," George sighed. "But if this has anything to do with monsters or ghosts, we're wasting our time."

The three friends climbed a red-carpeted staircase to the second floor. Quietly they followed the music to a door. It was open just a crack.

Nancy, Bess, and George peeked inside. An old-timey piano playing a lively tune stood in the middle of the room.

As Nancy looked closer, she gasped. The piano keys were moving up and down without a player!

"Do you see what I see?" Nancy hissed.

"Totally!" George said. "That piano is playing by itself!"

Chapter 4

SNARE AT THE FAIR

Nancy, Bess, and George raced down the stairs, out of the theater, and into the backseat of Mr. Drew's parked car.

"Write Nora Westcott's name on your suspect list, Nancy!" Bess insisted as they buckled their seatbelts. "Her curse is making those weird things happen at the theater!"

"That piano was weird," Nancy admitted. "But we don't know if a ghost was playing it or not."

"Remember when we thought that dog

Murray the Monster Mutt was a ghost?" George reminded them, "and he never was?"

"But I'll bet one clue led to another," Mr. Drew piped up as he drove away. "Right?"

Nancy and George both gave it a thought. Then they chorused, "Right."

"See?" Bess said. She pointed to Nancy's clue book open on her lap. "Add Nora Westcott's name to our list, Nancy, and write the word 'witch' next to it in big letters!"

Nancy did write Nora's name in her clue book. While Mr. Drew stopped for a red light he said, "It's a beautiful fall day today. Way too nice to be all work and no play."

"We like working on mysteries, Daddy," Nancy said.

"I know you also like the River Heights Fall Fair," Mr. Drew said.

Nancy, Bess, and George traded excited looks. Every year the Fall Fair had fun games, food— even a corn maze!

But when Nancy remembered their new case

she said, "We can't, Daddy. We have to solve this case before the *Twinkling Little Stars* people leave tomorrow night."

"But this is the Fall Fair, Nancy," Bess said.

"Even detectives need a candy apple break," George said. "With gooey caramel, crushed peanuts—"

"Okay, okay," Nancy said, her mouth watering. "Next stop—the Fall Fair!"

Mr. Drew drove to the fairgrounds. It was filled with colorful tents selling foods and crafts like scarecrows and carved jack-o'-lanterns.

"Caramel apples all around!" Mr. Drew said, buying apples for Nancy, Bess, and George. While he shopped at the market stalls, the girls played a pumpkin ring toss game. George won a sheet of stick-on Halloween tattoos.

A half hour went by before Nancy said, "Let's find my dad and ask if we can ride the carousel."

The girls strolled through the stalls looking for Mr. Drew. Instead they saw someone they didn't expect to see.

"Look!" George whispered. "It's Antonio!"

"He's one of our suspects," Nancy whispered back.

Antonio was standing at a vegetable stall. He was so busy examining carrots and celery, he didn't see the girls.

"That's weird," Bess whispered. "Antonio hates vegetables. He's always trading them for other stuff in the lunchroom."

Nancy suddenly noticed more. Something

inside the pocket of Antonio's hoodie was moving. She pointed it out to Bess and George, and they frowned.

"What do you think is in his pocket?" Bess hissed.

George shook her head. "We may be the Clue Crew," she said, "but I don't have a clue."

Nancy narrowed her eyes as they watched Antonio's wiggling pocket. "Looks like we have another mystery," she whispered. "What is Antonio hiding?"

The girls approached Antonio. Nancy decided to get right to the point. She tapped him on his shoulder and he whirled around.

"What do you have in your pocket, Antonio?" Nancy asked.

Antonio stared at the girls. "Candy corn," he blurted. "It's almost Halloween. Duh."

"Since when does candy corn move?" George asked, pointing to his pocket.

"Quit asking me about my pocket, okay?" Antonio exclaimed.

"Okay," George said. "There's something else we want to know anyway."

"What?" Antonio asked.

"Where were you at yesterday at five o'clock?" George demanded.

"None of your beeswax!" Antonio snapped. He dropped the celery he was holding, turned, and raced off.

"He's hiding something," Bess insisted, "and not just in his pocket!"

Nancy, Bess, and George chased Antonio through the pumpkin patch, zigzagging around bright orange pumpkins. Antonio was already out of the patch as he headed for the cornfield. After a quick glance back, Antonio darted through a narrow opening between the stalks.

"Don't let him get away!" Nancy said as she, Bess, and George raced between the stalks too.

Antonio was out of sight as the girls walked up a narrow path between two high walls of green cornstalks.

"Great," George groaned. "Antonio led us right into the corn maze."

The girls stopped and looked around. With so many twists and turns, the corn maze was like a giant puzzle!

"How are we going to find Antonio?" Nancy asked.

"Forget that, Nancy," Bess said. "How will we find our way out?"

Chapter 5

STALK THIS WAY

"We aren't lost," Nancy said. "Follow me!"

With stalks brushing their shoulders, Nancy led Bess and George to the end of the path. There they saw two more paths going in different directions.

"Now which way do we go?" Bess said.

"I know the way!" George said. "And it will lead us straight to Antonio."

She pointed to the ground and said, "Just follow the candy corn trail!"

Nancy smiled when she saw the candy.

"Antonio must have dropped it on his way through," she said.

"Sweet!" Bess exclaimed.

Nancy, Bess, and George followed the candy corn trail until it led them out of the maze. Standing in a clearing a few feet away was Antonio!

"How did you escape?" Antonio demanded. "Only I know the way out of that maze."

"Only the Clue Crew knows how to follow a trail," George said, "of candy corn!"

Antonio dug his hand into his pocket. "Great," he muttered. "There's a hole in it."

Nancy didn't care how Antonio lost his candy corn. She wanted answers!

"Antonio, did you ruin our props so we couldn't audition yesterday?" Nancy demanded.

"Because you couldn't audition yourself?" Bess added.

"I don't know what you're talking about," Antonio insisted.

"We heard you tell Peter you had a messy job to do," Nancy added.

"It was messy, all right," Antonio muttered. "It looked like a hamster food fight inside that cage."

Nancy, Bess, and George stared at Antonio.

"Hamster food fight?" Bess asked.

"Are you talking about Squeaky the hamster?" George asked. "Our class pet?"

"It was my turn to clean Squeaky's cage," Antonio replied. "I promised Ms. Ramirez I'd come back to school right after my audition."

Antonio then sighed and said, "You should have seen all the soggy veggies in Squeaky's cage. Gross."

Veggies? Nancy's eyes lit up as something clicked.

"Hamsters love eating veggies," Nancy told Antonio, "and you don't."

"What are you talking about?" Antonio asked.

"You were looking at vegetables before," Nancy said. "Were those vegetables for Squeaky?"

Antonio clapped his hand over his pocket. "Are you saying I took Squeaky?" he demanded. "He's not in my house, if that's what you're thinking!"

"I'm thinking he's in your pocket," George said, folding her arms across her chest. "Chewing candy corn and a big hole!"

Antonio rolled his eyes. He reached into his pocket and pulled out—

"Squeaky!" the girls cried in unison.

"I borrowed Squeaky for the weekend," Antonio said, holding the little brown-and-white hamster. "I didn't want my mom to find him in my room, so I brought him here."

"Does Ms. Ramirez know you borrowed Squeaky?" George asked.

"No," Antonio admitted. "I took Squeaky out after she inspected the cage."

With a shrug, Antonio said, "I always wanted a hamster—even if it was for only two days."

Nancy glanced over at Bess and George. She had a feeling they were thinking the same thing she was. Antonio did clean Squeaky's cage on Friday afternoon. So he couldn't have been at Rags 'n' Gags.

"Why don't you let us take Squeaky back to school, Antonio?" Nancy said. "Mr. Finney, the custodian, is there on Saturdays."

Nancy tilted her head and said, "Unless you want to return Squeaky yourself and tell Mr. Finney why he wasn't in his cage."

Antonio held Squeaky out to the girls. "Take him," he said. "I didn't know hamsters could be so messy. Or chew holes in pockets!"

"Thanks," Nancy said, taking Squeaky.

"And you can keep the veggies you were buying, Antonio," Bess said with a smile. "They're good for you!"

Nancy, Bess, and George found Mr. Drew watching a pumpkin carving demonstration. They asked him to drive them to the River Heights Elementary School.

"School?" Mr. Drew asked. "On Saturday?"

"Not for us, Daddy," Nancy said, holding up the hamster. "For Squeaky!"

Mr. Drew drove the girls from the fairgrounds to the school. They would walk home after they dropped off Squeaky.

Nancy, Bess, and George each had the same rules. They could walk anywhere as long as it was no more than five blocks and as long as they were together. Together was more fun anyway!

"Hi, girls," Mr. Finney greeted them at the door. "What brings you to school today?"

"We're bringing Squeaky back to his cage, Mr. Finney," Nancy said holding out the hamster.

"Back?" Mr. Finney asked. "How . . . ?"

"It's a long story, Mr. Finney," George said.

On the way to their classroom Nancy noticed a big banner hanging across the hall. It read, WELCOME HOME, LUCY O'TOOLE!

"I put that banner up this morning," Mr. Finney explained, "in case Lucy wants to visit her old school."

"Do you remember Lucy when she went to school here, Mr. Finney?" Nancy asked.

"I'm afraid I do," Mr. Finney said with a little smile. "Lucy used to get into a lot of trouble when she was here."

"Trouble?" Nancy asked with surprise.

"What kind of trouble?" Bess asked.

"Now Lucy is famous for her jokes," Mr. Finney explained. "But back then she was famous for mischievous pranks."

Nancy, Bess, and George traded stunned looks. Did Mr. Finney just say 'pranks'?

Chapter

PRANKS A LOT!

"You mean she played tricks on people, Mr. Finney?" Nancy asked.

Mr. Finney nodded. "Lucy played practical jokes on everyone—even the teachers," Mr. Finney replied. "She once dropped a goldfish in the principal's water bottle!"

"No way!" George exclaimed.

"Lucy glued nickels on the floor so nobody could pick them up," Mr. Finney went on. "She would stick silly signs on kids' backs without them knowing."

"Lucy is funny," Nancy said. "But those tricks don't sound funny to me."

"Or to me," Bess agreed. "Were Lucy's friends practical jokers too?"

Mr. Finney looked sad as he shook his head. "Lucy didn't have many friends because of her pranks," he said. "Nobody wanted to go to her parties, either."

"I don't blame them," George said. "Who would want to find goldfish in the strawberry punch bowl?"

Mr. Finney unlocked the classroom door.

"We'll take it from here, Mr. Finney," Nancy said as she, Bess, and George filed inside. "Thanks for your help."

"And the dish on Lucy!" George added.

The girls went straight to the cage in the back of the classroom. Nancy gently put Squeaky inside. The little hamster seemed thrilled to be home as he scurried into his exercise wheel.

"I'm glad we brought Squeaky back," Bess said.

"So am I," Nancy said. "What Mr. Finney just told us is big news!"

George rubbed her chin thoughtfully. "So Lucy O'Toole liked playing tricks," she said. "I wonder if she played a few tricks in the theater prop room yesterday morning."

"Lucy told us she wanted to do everything she did as a kid," Nancy said. "Maybe some of those things are pranks!"

"I can't believe Lucy would mess up our auditions," Bess admitted. "She's famous!"

"Famous for causing trouble," George said.

Nancy sat down at the nearest desk. She opened her clue book, crossed Antonio's name off her suspect list, and added Lucy's.

"We have to find out if Lucy was at Rags 'n' Gags Friday afternoon," Nancy said, "and in the prop room early this morning."

"I found a judge's badge in the prop room," Bess said excitedly. "Maybe it was Lucy's."

Nancy turned to the hamster cage. "Thanks, Squeaky!" she said with a smile.

"Why are you thanking him?" George asked.

"My dad always says that one clue can lead to another," Nancy explained. "Squeaky led us to Mr. Finney, who led us to Lucy O'Toole!"

Nancy, Bess, and George walked from their school to Rags 'n' Gags, just a few blocks away. The store's window was filled with Halloween masks, costumes, and party supplies.

The girls filed into the store. They were greeted by a teenage boy dressed up like Robin Hood. He was handing out cardboard glasses to everyone who entered.

"What are these?" George asked.

"Complimentary Ghost Goggles," the boy said, giving a pair to Nancy, Bess, and George. "In case you're on the lookout for ghosts."

"Right now we're on the lookout for the owner of the store," Nancy said.

"That would be Hank," the boy said. He

pointed to a man wearing a giant fake cheese wedge on his head. The man carried a stack of packaged costumes as he rushed about.

Nancy, Bess, and George pushed through the crowd of Halloween shoppers to Hank.

"Excuse me, Hank?" Nancy called.

"Sorry, girls," Hank called over his shoulder. "If you want a costume, take a number and wait your turn."

"We already have our costumes for Halloween," Bess said with a grin. "We're going as the three witch sisters."

"Yeah," George said, "we just want to know if—"

"You still have to get a ticket with a number on it," Hank said. He held up a package and called out, "Okay, who wanted the zombie superhero?"

"Not zombie superhero!" a boy said. "Zombie ninja!"

A girl stepped up to Hank. "And I wanted a rubber bat," she said, holding up a fake critter with a long tail. "This is a rubber rat!"

Hank grumbled, "Okay, okay. Be right back. Number nineteen, you're on deck!"

Nancy, Bess, and George walked over to the ticket machine on the counter. The number of the next ticket was forty-two!

"We'd have to wait forever to question Hank," Nancy sighed.

"We don't have forever," George complained. "It's getting late and we have to find out if Lucy was shopping here!"

Suddenly Bess flashed a smile. "Maybe we won't have to ask Hank if Lucy was here," she said.

"What do you mean?" Nancy asked.

"See for yourself," Bess said. She pointed to a

picture hanging on the wall behind the counter. The glossy picture was of a familiar person making a funny face.

When Nancy realized who it was, she gasped. "Omigosh, you guys," she said. "That's Lucy O'Toole!"

Chapter

7

HAUNTED HOUSE CALL

Nancy, Bess, and George slipped behind the counter for a better look.

"Lucy wrote something on her picture," Nancy pointed out. "It says, 'To Hank, Thanks for a ton of stuff! Cheers, Lucy!'"

"Wow!" George exclaimed. "You know what that means?"

"It means Lucy O'Toole did buy stuff here," Nancy said. "A ton of stuff!"

"But how do we know she bought rubber spiders, sneezing powder, and Bubble Blast?" Bess asked as they walked out from behind the counter.

Nancy could see Hank, surrounded by kids still yelling out their costume choices.

"We'd better not ask Hank," Nancy said. "Why don't we ask Lucy O'Toole instead?"

"Lucy said she was staying with her mother, but where is their house?" Bess asked.

"On O'Toole Street," George replied. "Mayor Strong named the street after her about a year ago."

"Of course! O'Toole Street is on our way home," Nancy said. "If Lucy did buy a ton of stuff here, maybe she'll have a ton of answers."

Nancy, Bess, and George squeezed their way out of the store and walked up Main Street. Along the way they saw a smaller crowd of kids standing in front of an apple cider cart.

Some kids seemed to be whispering excitedly. A few teenagers held their phones high above the crowd to take pictures.

"What's going on at the cider cart?" George asked.

Nancy was curious too. "Let's check it out," she said.

The girls walked to the cart. There was just one kid buying apple cider, and it was Cookie Sugarman!

Cookie was standing with Sherry, the producer of *Twinkling Little Stars*. But this time the sweetest star in Hollywood didn't look so sweet. . . .

"Where's the cinnamon?" Cookie shouted to

the man behind the cart. "Apple cider isn't apple cider without cinnamon!"

Then Cookie began blinking quickly before smiling. "I'll bet it's quite yummy without the cinnamon, sir," she said sweetly. "Thank you, oh so very much!"

Sherry whisked Cookie away. The man behind the apple cider cart looked confused as he shook his head.

"She went from being sour to sweet pretty fast," George pointed out.

"At least we know the *Twinkling Little Stars* people are still in River Heights," Nancy pointed out.

"As long as they are, we can still save the auditions!" Bess said.

Nancy, Bess, and George walked the few blocks to O'Toole Street. They stopped at a blue house at the end of the block.

"Are we sure this is Lucy's house?" Bess asked.

"Does that answer your question?" George

asked. She pointed to the mailbox. Flashing from the top was a bright neon sign that said LUCY'S FAN MAIL.

The girls walked up to the house. Nancy reached out and rang the doorbell. Instead of a bell they heard a deep voice say, "Enter . . . if you dare!"

"Maybe we shouldn't go inside," Bess said.

"Maybe we can e-mail Lucy. Or call her on the phone—"

"No, Bess," Nancy said. "Questioning a suspect face-to-face is better than on the phone."

"The voice told us to enter," George said, "so let's enter."

Slowly George opened the door, first a crack, then wider.

"Lucy?" Nancy called through the door.

"Lucy's mother?" Bess called.

George stepped inside. Nancy and Bess followed until all three girls stood in a dark, gloomy entrance hall.

"Wow," Nancy said softly.

All around were black candles dripping wax. Draped across the walls and staircase banister were dusty cobwebs.

"Since when does Lucy live in a haunted house?" Bess whispered. "I told you we shouldn't have come inside."

"We're inside already," George said. "So let's look for Lucy."

George took a few steps forward. Her foot landed on a mat that made a weird *squeak, squeak, squeak* noise. Then—

"Eeeeee!" Bess shrieked.

Nancy screamed too as a bevy of bats dropped down around them—wings flapping!

"Bat attack!" George shouted. "Cover your heads! Cover your heads!"

Chapter

8

LUCY EXCUSE-Y

Nancy, Bess, and George swatted the bats as they ran toward the door. But before they could leave—

"More guests?" a voice said. "Awesome!" The girls froze, then turned around. Behind them was a woman wearing a jester's cap of bells. Behind her was a cowboy, a ballerina, a baker, and a human box of crayons!

"I see you met my batty friends," Lucy said. She pulled at one to make it bounce. "Pretty realistic for rubber, huh?"

"That's for sure," George agreed. She waved her arms around the room. "What's up with all this, Lucy?"

"I was just about to add eyeball ice cubes to the punch," Lucy said. "And then we're going to play pin the fang on the vampire!"

Lucy tilted her head to study the girls. "Hey . . . weren't you those three witches that auditioned today?" she asked.

"That was us," Nancy said.

"Until our brew blew," Bess said.

Lucy wiggled her head to make the bells ring. "Then happy early Halloween, witch sisters!" she said. "You came just in time for my party!"

"That's what this is?" Nancy asked. "A Halloween party?"

"Yes, and it's about time," Lucy said. "When I

went to River Heights Elementary School I was a bit of a jokester."

"A bit?" the crayon man scoffed.

"Nobody wanted to come to my parties back then," Lucy sighed. "So when I came back to River Heights, I decided to invite some old classmates for a do-over."

"Lucy is totally prank-free now!" the ballerina said with a smile.

"Except on Halloween!" the baker said, giving one bat a playful swat. "But that's cool."

"She's famous now, too," the cowboy piped in. "Who knew her jokes would make her a celebrity some day?"

"Here's one!" Lucy chuckled. "I threw a boomerang at a ghost—and it came back to haunt me!"

Lucy's friends laughed, but the girls traded looks. Was Lucy really prank-free? Or was this a joke too—on them?

"How do we know you don't pull practical jokes anymore?" Nancy asked. "Like those pranks that were pulled at the auditions this morning?"

Lucy seemed surprised. "You think I ruined the auditions?" she asked.

"It depends," George said. "Where were you at five o'clock yesterday afternoon?"

The baker raised her hand. "Lucy was with me," she said. "We went to see *Zombie Slime Monsters* at the River Plex yesterday. The show started at five o'clock."

"We got to the theater a bit earlier," Lucy added, "to buy some snacks."

"Snacks, huh?" George slowly, "So how did you like the special slime-green popcorn?"

"We didn't," Lucy answered. "The popcorn machine was out of order."

George's eyes lit up. "Correct!" she told Lucy. "You knew that the popcorn machine was broken, so you had to be at *Zombie Slime Monsters* on Friday!"

"What are you?" Lucy asked the girls. "Some kind of kid detectives?"

"Correct again!" George said.

"We are detectives, Lucy," Nancy said, "and

we're glad you weren't at Rags 'n' Gags planning all that mean stuff."

"So I guess instead of being at the scene of the crime," Lucy joked, "I was at the scene of the slime!"

Everyone laughed. But when Nancy looked at Bess, she seemed puzzled.

"Lucy, if you weren't in the store," Bess asked, "why was your signed picture there?"

"I was at Rags 'n' Gags on Thursday buying neat things for this party," Lucy explained. "I've been in River Heights since Wednesday."

"And I'm loving every minute," a voice said.

Nancy, Bess, and George turned to see a kindly gray-haired woman dressed up like Mother Goose. She rubbed her hands together and said, "Okay! Who's ready to bob for shrunken heads?"

"Thanks, Mom!" Lucy said. She turned to the girls and asked, "You'll be staying for the party too, right?"

"Thanks, Lucy," Nancy said with a smile, "but we'd better go home now."

"But first," Bess said, pulling out the judge's badge, "maybe you dropped this in the Heights Theater prop room. You were one of the judges."

Lucy looked at the badge, then shook her head. "My badge is upstairs on my dresser," she said. "I'm sure of it."

As the girls left the house, Bess slipped the badge back into her pocket. "This badge must belong to Nathan," she said.

Nancy crossed Lucy's name off her suspect list and said, "We can give Nathan his badge on our way home. The Heights Theater is only a few blocks away."

But George didn't look very eager. "Why bother?" she sighed. "It's late Saturday afternoon and we still haven't found out who ruined the auditions."

Nancy knew time was running out for finding the theater prankster—but she refused to give up!

"We still have one day before the *Twinkling Little Stars* people go back to Hollywood," Nancy said.

"And one whole suspect," Bess said. "Nora Westcott—the witch of the Heights Theater."

"Give me a break, Bess," George groaned.

"I don't think the piano was played by a ghost, Bess," Nancy said. "I'm sure there was a reason for it."

The girls reached the Heights Theater. But when Nancy tried to open the door, it was locked.

"The theater must be closed for the day," Nancy said. "Let's give Nathan his badge tomorrow."

Nancy was just about to turn from the door, when she felt Bess grab her arm.

"What is it, Bess?" Nancy asked.

"There it is again!" Bess said.

"What?" George asked.

"The piano!" Bess hissed. "Listen!"

Nancy and George listened, then looked up.

The music seemed to be coming from an upstairs window. Behind the half-open window was a group of shadowy figures. As the girls looked closer, they noticed more.

"Holy cannoli!" George exclaimed.

Waving their arms and dancing to the music were a mummy, a vampire, a werewolf, and some kind of green creature that looked like a ghost!

"Bess, George," Nancy whispered, "are those monsters?"

Chapter 9

MONSTER BASH

The girls stared up at the window. The monsters and the ghost were still dancing up a storm!

"Should we go inside?" George asked.

Bess shook her head, her eyes wide. "I'm not going in there," she said. "No way!"

"You wanted to make Nora a suspect, Bess," Nancy reminded her. "She definitely is one now. So we have to find out more."

"I know," Bess said. "But can we come back when it's not so dark and creepy?"

"Let's come back tomorrow morning," Nancy agreed. "I'm sure Nathan will be here, so we won't be alone."

"And let's bring those Ghost Goggles we got at Rags 'n' Gags!" George said, then quickly added, "Not that I believe in ghosts . . . or monsters."

"I've never had pumpkin soup, Daddy," Nancy said as her father stirred the big pot on the kitchen stove. "But I'll bet it's yummy!"

"Hope so," Mr. Drew said. "I made it with foods I bought at the Fall Fair today."

Nancy was helping Hannah Gruen set the kitchen table for two. "Why aren't you eating dinner with us tonight, Hannah?" she asked.

Hannah smiled as she folded a napkin. She had been the Drews' housekeeper ever since Nancy was only three years old. But Hannah took such good care of Nancy that she was almost like a mother to her.

"We're ordering in dinner at my book club

meeting tonight," Hannah explained. "But save some soup for me."

"Sure, Hannah," Nancy said, staring down at the table. She tried to remember what side the spoon went on, but her mind was on something else.

"Daddy? Hannah?" Nancy asked slowly. "Have you guys ever heard of Nora Westcott?"

Hannah nodded and said, "She was an actress."

"Was she also . . . a witch?" Nancy asked.

"She sure was!" Hannah said with a smile. "A very famous witch, actually."

Nancy stared at Hannah. "She was? Really?"

"I'll tell you more about Nora tomorrow, Nancy," Hannah said. "I don't want to be late for my book club."

Hannah waved goodbye and left the kitchen. Nancy wanted to tell her dad what she saw at the theater, but he was too busy.

"Soup's ready!" Mr. Drew announced.

So am I, Nancy thought. Ready to check out the Heights Theater tomorrow—and those monsters!

"Yes!" George cheered as she opened the door. "The theater is open."

It was Sunday morning and the girls had returned to the Heights Theater. They would give Nathan his badge and then investigate the second floor for monsters and ghosts.

"Let's not tell Nathan what we saw yesterday," George told Nancy and Bess. "He's too sure there are no ghosts or monsters in this theater."

But when they reached Nathan's office, they saw that no one was inside. Bess pointed to Nathan's jacket hanging from a hook on the door.

"Nathan's badge is pinned to his jacket," Bess said. "If he didn't lose the one I found—who did?"

The girls' thoughts were interrupted by the sound of piano music and stomping feet upstairs.

"Do you hear that?" Nancy murmured, staring up at the ceiling.

"It's them," Bess whispered. "It's the monsters and ghosts."

"And that creepy piano that plays itself," George said. "I'm sure of it!"

"We can't be sure unless we see for ourselves," Nancy said. "Let's go upstairs."

"Okay, but not without our Ghost Goggles!" George insisted.

The Clue Crew slipped on the cardboard goggles. They climbed the stairs and followed the music and stomping to a room. The door was closed.

Bess began waving her arms in front of her. "These silly goggles," she complained. "They're making everything look bigger and greener!"

Bess's hands suddenly brushed up against the door. As it swung open, the music stopped. The girls gulped as they stared into the room. Staring back at them were the werewolf, the vampire, the mummy, and a green creature that looked like a ghost!

"Monsters!" Bess squeaked.

The fuzzy-faced werewolf with pointy teeth stepped toward the door. "Hi," he said. "Cool glasses!"

Nancy stared at the werewolf through her Ghost Goggles. Then she tried looking at him without them. That's when something came in big and clear—something dangling underneath his fuzzy chin. Looking closer, Nancy knew exactly what it was!

"You guys," Nancy said, "I don't think they're monsters or ghosts."

"Why not?" George asked, taking her own goggles off.

"The werewolf is wearing a mask," Nancy said, "with a Rags 'n' Gags price tag!"

The werewolf pulled off the mask to reveal a friendly human face. "Did I forget to cut off the tag?" he said. "Silly me!"

"Don't get me started on masks," the green ghost complained. "This thing is hotter than my flat iron on a bad hair day."

The ghost pulled off her mask to reveal her face—sweaty but friendly!

"You're all human?" Bess asked. She was goggle-free now too.

"Only until we star in our upcoming show," the mummy said with a little tap dance. "*Guys and Ghouls!*"

"Opening night is in a week," the werewolf said. "As you can see by our costumes, we're in dress rehearsals."

The actors introduced themselves. The werewolf was Randy, the green ghost was Crystal, the vampire was Ken, and the mummy was Liz.

"Come in and check out our pianola," Liz said, waving the girls into the room.

"A pianola is a self-playing piano," Randy explained. "It will be in our show too."

Liz flicked a switch behind the piano. The keys began moving up and down.

"We saw it playing the other day!" Bess said.

"I must have forgotten to turn it off after rehearsal," Randy the werewolf sighed. "Silly me!"

Nancy was happy the monsters and ghosts weren't real. But she couldn't stop thinking about Nora and what Hannah said. . . .

"Have any of you heard of Nora Westcott?" Nancy asked. "We were told she was an actress who became a witch."

"You heard right," Ken said. "Nora left the theater to star in a big Hollywood movie, *Which Witch Is Which?*"

"Nora played the part of Rolanda," Liz said, "a very good witch!"

Nancy smiled at her friends and said, "So that explains it."

"Yeah," George said, smiling too. "Now who's going to explain it to Quincy Taylor?"

Crystal reached into her handbag on the piano bench. "Speaking of big stars," she said, "look who I saw in the prop room early Saturday morning."

Nancy stopped smiling to stare at Crystal. Did she just say 'the prop room early Saturday morning'? As in the time and place of the crime?

"Who was there, Crystal?" Nancy asked.

Crystal held up her phone to show a selfie. With her in the picture was a star. The sweetest star in Hollywood!

"Bess, George," Nancy gasped. "Do you see who I see?"

Clue Crew—and
YOU!

Join Nancy, Bess, and George in solving this mystery. Or turn the page to find out whodunit!

1. Nancy, Bess, and George ruled out Antonio, Lucy, and Nora's curse. Who else could have been in the prop room at the time of the crime? List your suspects on a piece of paper.

2. Clues like the judge's badge are super important. If the badge wasn't Lucy's or Nathan's, whose badge could it be? Write down your thoughts on a piece of paper.

3. Nancy, Bess, and George like writing clues and suspects in their clue book. What else could they write or draw to help them solve mysteries? Make a list of your ideas on a piece of paper.

Chapter 10

SWEET SURRENDER

"It's Cookie Sugarman!" George said.

"The sweetest star in Hollywood!" Bess added.

Nancy leaned closer to Crystal's phone for a better look. The date on the picture was Saturday. The time was eight-thirty a.m.!

"The cast of *Guys and Ghouls* uses a different prop room," Crystal explained. "I went into that room to find thread for a torn costume, and instead I found Cookie."

"Was Cookie there alone?" Nancy asked.

"She was," Crystal said. "Cookie looked surprised to see me, but she agreed to take a selfie."

"Did you stay with Cookie after the selfie?" Bess asked.

"No," Crystal said. "Cookie told me she had work to do, so I left."

"Now if you'll excuse us," Ken piped up nicely, "we have to rehearse our next number, 'Too Cool for Ghouls!'"

Nancy, Bess, and George thanked the actors and left. They had much to talk about as they walked down the stairs.

"Are we lucky or what?" George asked. "Crystal just gave us a great clue."

Nancy nodded and said, "Cookie was alone in the prop room on Saturday morning."

"Cookie was a judge, too," Bess pointed out. "So the badge I found in the prop room could have been hers."

As the girls reached the bottom of the stairs, Nancy shook her head in disbelief. "I can't believe

Cookie would ruin our auditions," she said. "She's so sweet!"

"She was pretty sour when we saw her buying apple cider," George pointed out. "Remember?"

All of a sudden the girls heard a loud—

"Ah-chooooo!"

Then another, and another—and another!

"It sounds like a kid," George said.

"A kid with a bad cold," Nancy added.

The girls followed the explosive sneezes to the prop room. Nancy knocked on the closed door lightly and called, "Are you okay?"

"Do you need a tissue?" Bess called too.

When no one answered, Nancy slowly opened the door. What they saw inside made their jaws drop. Standing with a spray can in her outstretched hands was Cookie!

"Don't take another step!" Cookie warned. "I've got a can of sneezing powder and I'm not afraid to use it!"

"Cookie, put the can down," Nancy said as she and her friends entered the prop room.

"What are you doing with sneezing powder, anyway?" George asked.

Still holding the can of Skeevy's sneezing powder, Cookie said, "I came to get my Rags 'n' Gags bag. The can fell out and the lid popped off. I've been sneezing my nose off ever since— Ah-choooo!"

"Why did you have a can of sneezing powder?" Bess asked.

"Yeah," George said, raising an eyebrow. "Seems like a weird thing to carry around."

Cookie stared wide-eyed at the girls. "Um . . . it's part of my Halloween costume," she blurted. "I'm going as . . . Sneezy of the Seven Dwarfs!"

"Nice try, Cookie," George said, before throwing her head back and sneezing herself.

Cookie grumbled under her breath as her hands, and the can of sneezing powder, fell to her sides.

"Cookie," Nancy said gently, "did you use stuff from Rags 'n' Gags to ruin the *Twinkling Little Stars* auditions?"

Cookie chewed on her lip, then said, "I guess I did."

"Well, that wasn't very sweet," Bess said.

"Sweet! Sweet!" Cookie groaned. "What am I—saltwater taffy?"

"You weren't very sweet at the apple cider cart yesterday," Bess pointed out.

"Yeah," George agreed. "That was some meltdown you had, Cookie."

"That's just it!" Cookie said, waving her arms. "Sometimes I'm sweet and sometimes I get a little moody. Just like any normal kid!"

Cookie gave a sigh and said, "Everyone expects me to be sweet. And I'm sick of it."

"Why are you sick of it?" Nancy asked.

"All I get are sweet parts in movies, like princesses with unicorns," Cookie explained. "The villains in movies are soooo cool!"

Nancy shot her friends a sideways glance. So that's what this was all about. To Cookie, being sweet was not so neat!

"I'll never get to play a villain because I'm just too good," Cookie said.

"So you ruined our props before the auditions," George asked, "just to see what it was like to be bad?"

"Bingo," Cookie sighed.

"Did it make you feel good?" Nancy asked.

"No way," Cookie admitted. "I felt awful when the auditions were called off and everyone was so sad."

Cookie nodded her chin at the Rags 'n' Gags bag. "That's why I came back to get my bag," she said. "I didn't want anyone to use that stuff ever again!"

Nancy, Bess, and George smiled at Cookie. They were glad she'd told the truth. And super glad the pieces of the puzzle had fallen into place!

"Do you think you'll tell Sherry what you did, Cookie?" George asked.

"Maybe the *Twinkling Little Stars* auditions can still go on!" Bess said excitedly.

Cookie sadly shook her head. "It's too late," she sighed. "We're going back to Hollywood tomorrow night."

"You'll never know unless you try!" Nancy said.

Cookie seemed to give it a thought as she carefully placed the can of sneezing powder back in the big bag.

"Okay, but I might need your help . . . ah . . . ah . . . ah-chooo!!" Cookie sniffed, then added, "And a lot of tissues!"

"You were right, Nancy," Bess said. "It wasn't too late to bring back the auditions!"

Nancy was so thrilled, she could do a hundred cartwheels. Cookie had told Sherry what she did and why. The producer decided they would fly back a day later. The auditions were held on Sunday and an extra day on Monday after school!

"I think we did a great job as the three witches this time," Nancy told her friends.

The girls were dressed head-to-toe in their costumes, waiting to hear who the winner was.

"Cookie did a great job apologizing, too," George said. "It was cool of her to let Hank from Rags 'n' Gags be a judge in her place."

"Cookie did a great job helping us with our brew, too!" Bess added with a smile. "Just a teeny drop of Bubble Blast did the trick!"

A hush fell over the theater as Mayor Strong walked to the microphone. Nancy, Bess, and George joined hands. This was it!

"You all did a fabulous job," the mayor announced. "But since only one act can perform on *Twinkling Little Stars*, the winner is . . . "

Nancy, Bess, and George squeezed hands tightly.

". . . Those acrobatic arachnids, Cirque du Crawl-ay!"

Nadine and the other dancers shrieked as they ran onstage. They were going to Hollywood to dance on *Twinkling Little Stars*!

"I'm happy for Nadine," Nancy admitted.

"Me too," Bess sighed, "but sad we won't be going to Hollywood."

"What could be better than three awesome witches?" George asked.

"I know!" Nancy said with a smile. "How about three awesome detectives?"

The Clue Crew traded a high five as they said together: "Bubble, bubble, toil and trouble—we solved this case on the double!"

Test your detective skills with even more Clue Book mysteries:

Nancy Drew Clue Book #11:
The Tortoise and the Scare

Nancy Drew stood in front of her science class with an index card in her hand. Her best friends, George Fayne and Bess Marvin, were sitting in the back row. She stared down at the card, wanting to give everyone a clue that was good, but not too good. She didn't want them to guess the answer right away.

"I'm tiny . . . ," she said. "And I have spines and short legs."

"Hmmm . . . ," Mrs. Pak, their teacher, murmured. She glanced around the class-room. "What could she be? Does anyone have any ideas?"

Jamal Jones's hand shot up in the air. He always got straight As and had guessed the last two correct answers. Nancy held her breath, wondering if he'd get it right.

"Are you a porcupine?" he asked.

"You're so close!" Nancy gave another clue, and she was sure he'd get it right this time. "I can roll up into a ball if I'm scared. . . ."

"Oh! You're a hedgehog!" Jamal cried.

"Very good!" Mrs. Pak said, taking the card from Nancy. It had hedgehog written on it in block letters. "This class is going to be so prepared for our field trip tomorrow. I'm sure all the guides at the River Heights Wildlife Center will be impressed."

Nancy took her seat next to her friends. Bess's long blond hair was pulled back in a ponytail as she leaned over her book. The World's Most Exotic Animals was open to the page about servals. The spotted cat looked like a cheetah with bunny ears. "Their ears are so cute," Bess said, pointing to the pictures. "They're so much bigger than their heads! I hope we get to see one tomorrow."

"I want to see a ball python," George said.

"Those are terrifying!" Bess whispered.

"And slimy," Nancy added.

George and Bess were cousins, but they couldn't have been more different. George had short brown hair and brown eyes, was athletic, and was not easily scared. Bess always feared the worst would happen, and Nancy had only ever seen her play sports in gym class. Together the three of them made up the Clue Crew. They worked together solving mysteries around River Heights. They'd even recovered a telescope that had been stolen from a local museum.

Harry and Liam McCormick went to the front of the class. They were identical twins, with orange hair and freckles, and they liked doing presentations together whenever Mrs. Pak would let them. They'd just moved to River Heights in September, and were obsessed with Antonio Elefano, the biggest prankster in Nancy's grade.

The twins were constantly doing things to try to impress him. Just the week before they'd climbed thirty feet up a tree trying to get his attention.

"Ummm . . . we're red," Liam said, staring at his card. "I mean I'm red."

"And we have giant wings!" Harry added.

Nancy thought they might be parrots . . . maybe sun conures, but that seemed too obvious. They'd been studying so many exotic animals that she sometimes got them mixed up. Was it possible they were scarlet macaws?

"I don't think we are red . . . ," Harry said quietly to his brother. "Aren't we blue?"

Mrs. Pak leaned over their shoulders to get a better view of their cards. "I think you're red and blue. And maybe a few other colors too."

"We're very colorful," Liam agreed.

George raised her hand. "You're a scarlet macaw."

"That's right! She's right," Liam said. He seemed excited that someone had guessed the correct answer, even though they were a bit confused about which bird the macaw was.

Mrs. Pak moved on to the next lesson, pulling up a video of a three-toed sloth on the screen in front of the class. The furry creature was swimming. As the rest of the class watched it paddle through the water, Nancy leaned over to her friends.

"Tomorrow is going to be a perfect day," she said. "There's supposed to be this cool courtyard at the wildlife center with a crazy playground and a hedge maze. And there's a gift shop where you can buy stuffed animals or these pens with floating parrots in them."

"Someone said they actually put the python around your neck," George whispered. "You can hold them!"

"George!" Nancy and Bess practically screamed. Then they broke into laughter, thinking of George with a giant snake hanging over her shoulders. Sometimes the things that totally creeped them out were the same things George loved.

"I don't think we've been somewhere this fun since . . . ," Bess trailed off, her eyes wide.

"Maybe ever," George added.

Nancy smiled, knowing it was true. The River Heights Wildlife Center was going to be their biggest adventure yet.

"You must be Mrs. Pak, and I'm guessing these are your exceptional science students!" A woman with curly black hair bounded down the front steps of the wildlife center. She was wearing khaki from head to toe—khaki shorts, a khaki shirt, and even khaki-colored socks. Her name tag read belinda.

"They are," Mrs. Pak said cheerfully. "We've been so excited to visit."

"Well come on in." The woman waved each of them inside one by one. "I'm Belinda, and I'm the founder of the River Heights Wildlife Center. I'll be taking care of you today. Before we get started

I wanted to tell you a little bit about the place, and you can meet the wonderful staff that makes magic happen around here."

Nancy followed Bess and George inside the center, which was a single-story building with a beautiful courtyard garden in the middle of it. There were already two other school groups there. The playground was crowded with kids and a group of moms with strollers. Nancy could hear animal noises echoing down the corridor. To the side of the garden, there was a huge playground and the hedge maze that Nancy had read about online. Two men in khaki uniforms were standing by the café and picnic tables.

"Come, sit down!" Belinda said, waving for the class to find spots at the picnic tables. "I want to tell you a little bit about what brought me here to the River Heights Wildlife Center."

Nancy and her friends sat on the bench closest to Belinda. She seemed like she was much younger than Nancy's parents. She had funny pins all over the front of her shirt. One said tou-

can play at that game and had a cartoon draw-
ing of a toucan. Another said toadally and had an
annoyed-looking toad on it.

"I'm so happy you all could come visit today,
because helping animals has become my life's pas-
sion," Belinda said. "I started rescuing abandoned
and injured animals when I was just a teenager.
I worked in a bird sanctuary after college, and
then I came here to the River Heights Wildlife
Center."

"Are all of your animals injured?" Lily Almond,
a girl with long black pigtails, asked. She was the
biggest animal lover in class. Nancy had been to
her house once for a school project and met her
two hamsters, one bunny, three dogs, and her
twenty-pound cat, Otis.

"Most of them were when they came in here,"
Belinda answered. "All of them needed our help.
Sometimes people buy animals and they don't
know what to do with them. Like our flying
squirrel, Bean. Someone bought him online and
didn't like how much time and effort it took to

take care of him. Or our wolf, Moonrise. People actually thought he was a dog, so they brought him home, and he was trouble . . . big trouble. He tore apart two couches and ate a hole in their door."

"We learned a lot about wolves," Jamal said excitedly.

"Yes, Mrs. Pak told me all about the lessons you've been doing lately." Belinda looked genuinely interested. "Do you know the difference between a wolf and a dog?"

"Wolves have fur on their bellies, and amber-colored eyes," Jamal said.

"And their ears stick straight up!" Lily chimed in.

"That's right," Belinda said. "We'll talk more above wolves and snakes and birds, but first I want to introduce you all to the wonderful staff here. Because we use so much of our donations to rescue and take care of our wildlife, many people who work here are volunteers. Bob has been volunteering the longest, for five years now."

A man with frizzy white hair stepped forward. He looked like he could have been someone's grandpa. "After I retired I thought it might be a fun thing to do. And I was right! I work with all the wildlife here, but I really love the capuchin monkeys. The kinkajou, too."

"The kinkajou . . . ?" Bess whispered to Nancy. Her brows furrowed.

Nancy remembered them from one of their textbooks, even though they didn't spend a lot of time talking about them. "It's like a tiny raccoon but it's honey-colored instead of gray. And it lives in trees."

The other man stepped forward after Belinda was done talking about Bob. He had long blond hair that came down to his shoulders. He wore rings on three of his fingers, and had a goatee.

"And this is Ocean," Belinda said, introducing him. "And yes—before you ask, that is his real name."

"She tells the truth!" Ocean laughed. "My parents were hippies. I grew up on a farm in California and I've always loved wildlife, especially reptiles. I have a California king snake named Steven and a tortoise named Bette. They're two of my best friends."

"A California king," George said to no one in particular. "Very cool."

"You'll meet Lisa in the gift shop, and Miles is coming in later," Belinda said. "Now let's start our tour, shall we? There are so many wonderful creatures here and so little time."

"Do you have pets?" Bess asked Belinda.

"I have two chinchillas at home," Belinda said, as she led the group back into the building. "I'd love to have more pets, but I take care of so many animals here, it feels like I already do. Now where should we start . . . ?" She looked down the right hallway, then down the left. "Are you ready to meet Rainbow?"

The class cheered in response. Belinda led them to a huge enclosure with sand and shrubs in it, and fresh produce scattered everywhere. A short wood fence surrounded the perimeter.

"It looks like a cabbage exploded," Nancy whispered to Bess. "What's in there?"

"Okay everybody, find a space along the outside of the fence to look for Rainbow. She might be hard to spot at first, but look closely," Belinda directed. She waited, watching the class' faces.

Everyone lined up along the fence and peered into the enclosure.

"I see her . . . ," Lily said. Then a few more kids agreed.

Nancy narrowed her eyes and finally saw a large tortoise behind a shrub. She was all the way in the back of the habitat. Her shell was brown and dark green, so she blended in with the sand and leaves around her.

"Rainbow will always have a very special place in my heart," Belinda said, staring at the tortoise. "She was my very first rescue here at the wildlife center. An older woman had her as a pet, but when she moved she just left Rainbow in her yard with a rotting pile of vegetables. The new owners found her and, well, they called me."

Nancy stared down at the tortoise. She felt really sad for the animal. She had to admit, it was awful that someone had just left Rainbow there all alone. What would have happened if no one found her?

"On the day I went and got her," Belinda went on, "there was the most spectacular rainbow in the sky."

"And that's how she got her name," Mrs. Pak said. She smiled, even though that part was a little obvious. It was clear Mrs. Pak loved each one of Belinda's stories.